For Nettie

BLOOMSBURY CHILDREN'S BOOKS
Bloomsbury Publishing Inc., part of Bloomsbury Publishing Plc
1385 Broadway, New York, NY 10018

BLOOMSBURY, BLOOMSBURY CHILDREN'S BOOKS, and the Diana logo
are trademarks of Bloomsbury Publishing Plc

First published in Great Britain in August 2021 by Bloomsbury Publishing Plc
Published in the United States of America in March 2022
by Bloomsbury Children's Books

Bloomsbury books may be purchased for business or promotional use. For information on bulk purchases please contact
Macmillan Corporate and Premium Sales Department at specialmarkets@macmillan.com

Library of Congress Cataloging-in-Publication Data
available upon request
LCCN: 2021026250
ISBN 978-1-5476-0822-5 (hardcover)
ISBN 978-1-5476-0823-2 (e-book) • ISBN 978-1-5476-0824-9 (e-PDF)

Art created digitally using a combination of natural media brushes in Procreate on an iPad and a Wacom drawing tablet with Adobe Photoshop on an iMac
Book design by Goldy Broad • Typeset in Appareo Medium
Printed and bound in China by Leo Paper Products, Heshan, Guangdong
2 4 6 8 10 9 7 5 3 1

To find out more about our authors and books visit www.bloomsbury.com and sign up for our newsletters.

TILDA
TRIES AGAIN

TOM PERCIVAL

BLOOMSBURY
CHILDREN'S BOOKS
NEW YORK   LONDON   OXFORD   NEW DELHI   SYDNEY

Tilda's world was just
as she liked it.

She had her friends,

her books,

and her toys.

Everything was
just right.

Until one day, Tilda's world turned . . .

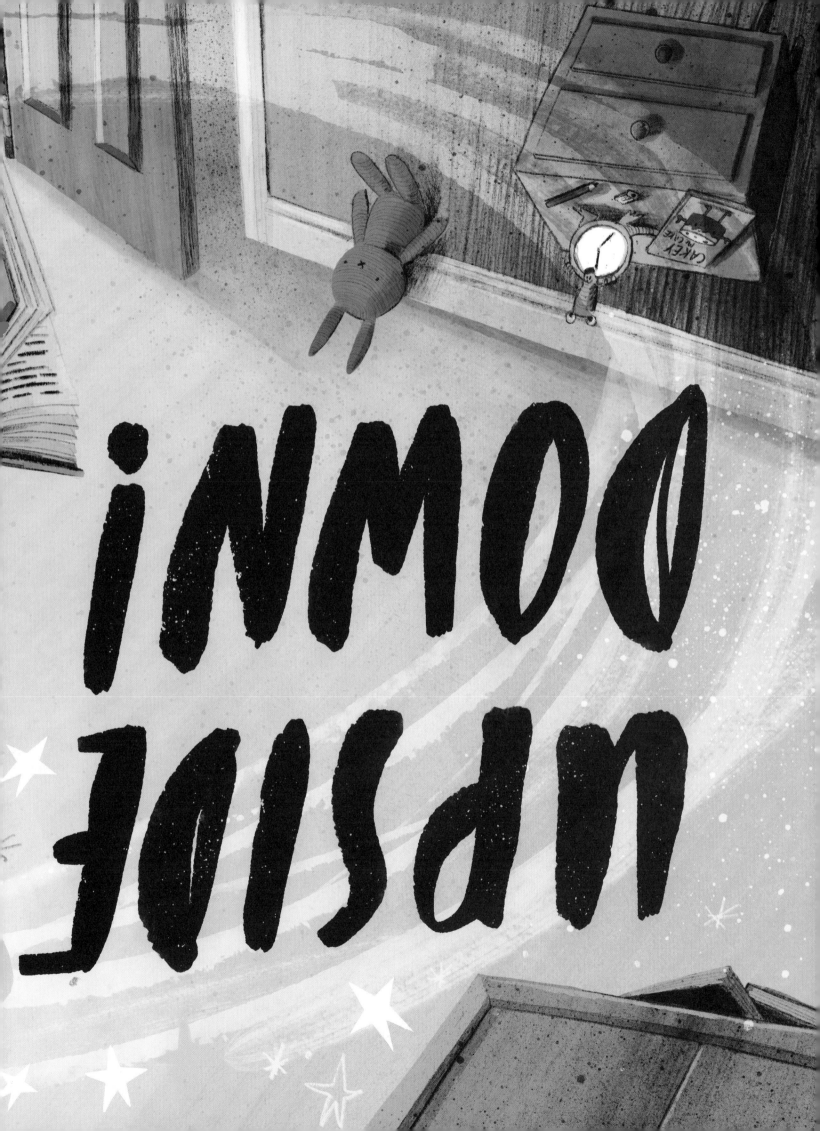

All of a sudden, everything was topsy-turvy.

And *nothing* felt right anymore.

Things that had once seemed simple
now felt *incredibly* difficult.

Tilda didn't feel like seeing her friends.

In fact, she didn't feel like
doing anything.

Everything just seemed
TOO hard.

Eventually, Tilda gave up
and decided to do . . .

Then one day, Tilda saw a ladybug
stuck on its back. Its tiny legs
waggled in the air.

"Poor little thing," she said.
"You're all topsy-turvy . . .

just like me."

As Tilda tried to work out how to help,
the ladybug wriggled and struggled.

It was no use.
Tilda's heart sank.

But then, the ladybug
tried again,

and again,

and again.

Until at last . . .

it flew free!

Tilda thought about this.
The ladybug hadn't given up . . .

so neither would she!

She found her toy blocks and tried
building something.

It worked!

Tilda started to feel
a bit better.

After that, she tried reading her favorite funny
book and laughed until her tummy ached.

Then she went out to play in the yard.

Everything still felt *very* strange.
But Tilda tried her best.

And the more Tilda *tried*,
the more she found
she COULD do.

Although there was one thing
that still felt too hard . . .

Tilda paused at the edge of the park
and watched her friends.
She almost left . . .

but then Tilda remembered the ladybug.

Could *she* be brave?
Could *she* keep trying?

Tilda decided that she *could*!

And it was the best decision
she ever made.

Even though her world
was still a little topsy-turvy,
Tilda felt she could cope.

And because she felt she could cope,
her world seemed less topsy-turvy!

From that day on, whenever Tilda's world felt
a bit wobbly, she just tried her best.

And if that didn't work?

Tilda tried **again**!

Dear Reader,

Sometimes things can feel hard, like *nothing* is working out. That's what happens to Tilda in this story. But while giving up might feel like the easiest option, it never *really* helps. Here are a few tips to help *you* keep going!

- ➤ Whenever you're faced with a challenge that seems too hard, break it down into smaller chunks. You'll get there in the end!
- ➤ Try listing all the things that make you feel happy and find time to do them! Doing things that you enjoy makes you feel good.
- ➤ Look after yourself! Get enough sleep and exercise, and eat healthy food. Problems often seem less upsetting after a good night's sleep.

But remember that we *all* have setbacks and sometimes, things just *don't* work out. If that happens, it's natural to feel a bit low. No matter what you're feeling, remember that it always helps to talk about it. Be open, be honest, be YOU!

Love,

TOM

Here's an organization that offers resources if you're interested in learning more: **childmind.org**